ISBN 13: 9781634892469

Printed in the United States of America

First Printing: 2019

23  22  21  20  19          5  4  3  2  1

Book design by Patrick Maloney


Wise Ink Creative Publishing
807 Broadway St. NE, Suite 46
Minneapolis, MN 55413

# Ely Eagle Learns to Fly

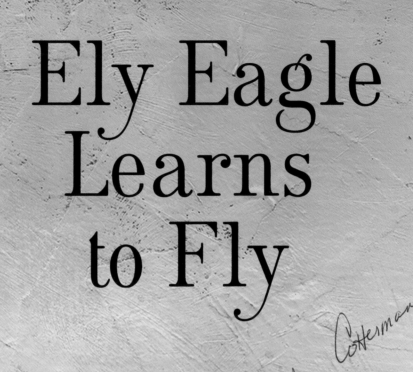

by DEBRA
COTTERMAN

*Debra Cotterman*

illustrated by
SHAWN McCANN

To Carole, for twenty years of
encouragement and support,
and to Hogan and Michael—
so proud of how you fly!

Ely Eagle was getting ready to travel
with her family through the big, big woods
to visit her grandparents' nest.
But Ely had a big problem . . .

Ely had never
flown before.

Ely thought of her friend Scandia Squirrel.
Scandia traveled through the big woods
every day. Maybe she could help.

So, Ely found Scandia high in the trees,
jumping from branch to branch.

"Scandia!" Ely called. "I need to get through the big, big woods to visit my grandparents. Do you know how I can get there without flying?"

"Yes!" said Scandia. "Jump from branch to branch like I do! You'll be there in no time."

Ely hopped onto a low branch. She tried to jump to the next one, but without a tail, she couldn't balance. She slipped off the branch and landed on the ground with a *thud!*

"I don't think I can get to my grandparents' nest by jumping, but thanks for helping me!" she said as she picked leaves out of her wings.

Then Ely remembered her friend
Lindstrom "Lindy" Loon.
Lindy traveled on
the river all day.
Ely headed down
to the water.

"Lindy!" she called. "I need to get through the big, big woods to visit my grandparents. Do you know how I can get there without flying?"

"Yes!" said Lindy. "Swim like I do! Just sit on the water and use your feet to paddle."

Ely stepped into the river. She tried to paddle, but without webbed feet, she couldn't move and her wings splashed water all over!

"I don't think I can get to my grandparents' nest by swimming, but thanks for helping me!" she said as she shook the water off her wings.

Then Ely remembered her friend Willmar Wolf. Willmar could run faster than anyone in the forest. Ely found Willmar playing with his best friend, Fergus Fox.

"Willmar!" she called. "I need to get through the big, big woods to visit my grandparents. Do you how I can get there without flying?"

"Yes!" said Willmar. "Run like me or hop like Fergus! Just put your head down and go as fast as you can!"

Ely lowered her head and tucked her wings close. She tried to lunge forward, but without strong, swift legs like her friends had, she fell forward into a bramble bush.

"I don't think I can get to my grandparents' nest by running or hopping, but thanks for helping me!" she said, brushing the brambles out of her wings.

Ely was walking away when her friend Mankato Moose walked by.

"Mankato," said Ely. "I need to get through the big, big woods to visit my grandparents. Do you know a way I can get there without flying?"

"Yes!" said Mankato. "I stand tall when I walk, and I don't have to worry about bramble bushes. Jump up onto my antlers and I will carry you."

Ely hopped up and Mankato strolled into the woods.

But up on Mankato's back, branches bumped Ely in the face. She tried to push them away with her wings, but feathers were not as strong as antlers.

Finally, she shouted, "Stop!"

"I don't think I can get to my grandparents' nest by walking or riding, but thanks for helping me!" Ely said as she jumped to the ground.

Ely Eagle sat down on an old tree trunk.
She was very sad and worried.

But then, Ely's friend Bemidji Bear
came and sat down beside her.
He had watched all the
ways Ely had tried to travel.

"Oh, Bemidji," said Ely, "I need to get through the big, big woods to visit my grandparents. All my friends have tried to show me the special ways they travel, but my wings always got in the way!"

"Well," said Bemidji, "maybe those wings *are* your special way to travel."

Ely thought about that for a minute.

"You're right!" she said. "If I flew to my grandparents', I wouldn't fall off a branch or get wet or get brambles and branches in my feathers. Maybe flying is the best way for me to travel after all."

There was just one problem.
"My brothers and sisters go so high,"
said Ely. "I've never even flown."

"I know who can help with that," said Bemidji.
Bemidji went back into the woods and
returned with all Ely's friends.

Wilmar and Fergus climbed up
onto Mankato's shoulders.

Then Bemidji picked up Ely in his big paws
and climbed up with Scandia and Lindy.

Bemidji lifted Ely until she sat
right on the top of Wilmar's head.

Then Mankato stood tall, raising
Ely high into the air.

Ely could see the tops of the trees
and across the big, big woods.
And she could see her family
soaring above her.

"Go ahead, Ely," said Bemidji.
"You can do it!"

"You can fly! You can fly!"
shouted her friends.

And with one big jump,
Ely soared into the sky
to join her family.

"Hurray!" everybody shouted.

Ely's mother swooped close to her.
"Oh, Ely," she said, "I am so
proud you are flying with us!"

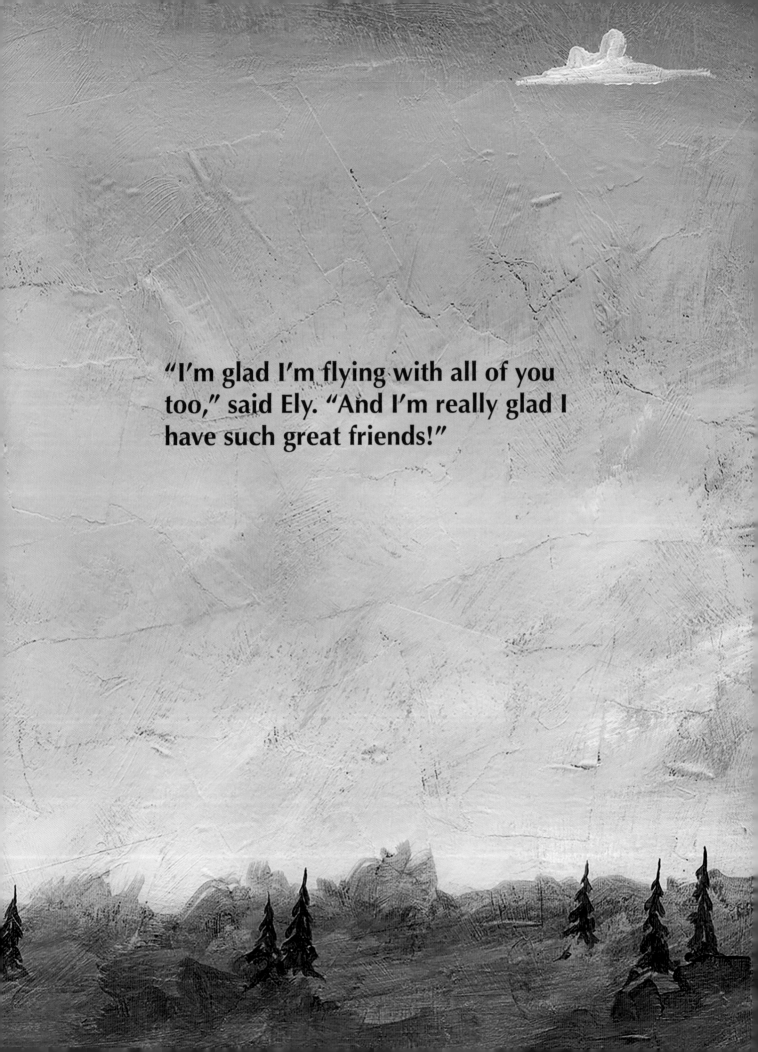

"I'm glad I'm flying with all of you too," said Ely. "And I'm really glad I have such great friends!"

**Debra Cotterman** is a life-long Minnesotan who still (kind of) believes that animals talk to each other when people aren't looking. In the seventh grade she wrote an essay stating she wanted to be a writer when she grew up, and here, only fifty years later, is her first book. Debra is a mom, a bookstore owner, and a reader and collector of children's books. She currently lives in Apple Valley, Minnesota.

**Shawn McCann** is an artist who loves to explore the relationship of art, space, and interaction. Having graduated the Minneapolis College of Art and Design with a BFA, Shawn has grown into a multi-media, multi-disciplinary artist whose work explores color, texture, form, and content.

Ely Eagle and all her friends first came to life in the
imagination of creator and entrepreneur Carole Howe.

You can visit a life-sized sculpture of these whimsical
animals at Ms. Howe's store, Minnesota State of Nice,
in the Minneapolis–St. Paul International Airport.

The happy faces of Ely, Lindy, Mankato, and all the rest
were the inspiration for this story.